THE LAST CONFESSION OF JOSEPH DELLA REINA

by

Barak A. Bassman

TELEMACHUS PRESS

This book is a work of fiction. Names, characters, places and incidents are either the product of the author's imagination or are used fictitiously. Any resemblance to actual persons, living or dead, or to actual events or locales is entirely coincidental.

THE LAST CONFESSION OF JOSEPH DELLA REINA

Cover designed by Telemachus Press, LLC

Cover art:
Copyright © iStock/166244773_nicoolay

Published by Telemachus Press, LLC
http: //www.telemachuspress.com

ISBN: 978-1-948046-16-9 (eBook)
ISBN: 978-1-948046-17-6 (paperback)
ISBN: 978-1-948046-18-3 (hardback)

Library of Congress Control Number: 2018945333

FICTION / General
FICTION / Folklore

Version 2018.05.21

Table of Contents

The Last Confession of
Joseph della Reina

I. Haman Is Dying

The Jews of the Duchy of W. rejoiced: Their persecutor was on his deathbed. For many years this man, one of the Duke's wealthiest courtiers, had spread the most terrible lies about the Duchy's Jews, leading many of them to lose their heads and their property. The Jews of W. had fasted and prayed many times for their deliverance from this enemy.

And now there had come the joyous news: This new Haman was dying, alone on some country estate in a black forest. In the Great Synagogue of the Duchy's largest town, liquor flowed freely and there was riotous singing and dancing. Groups of mischievous teenage boys wandered about town performing impromptu Purim plays about how the wicked slanderer had fallen and was reaping the due reward for his crimes. Bakers liberally handed out sweet pastries to eager children. Even the bleating of the goats seemed to have a festive ring.

But as night fell, the Jews began to worry that perhaps they had celebrated too soon. Four knights in black armor and a tar-black carriage halted in front of the Great Synagogue. The coachman, with a look of grim determination in his eyes, entered the vestibule of the synagogue and banged a heavy metal rod against the floor until the half-drunk Jews, with their smiles fading, fell silent. The coachman announced that the wicked one had sent him to summon the town's rabbi. The armed men accompanying the coach were prepared to compel compliance with the summons by force, but His Lordship hoped that would not be necessary.

Dozens of trembling, terrified eyes, suddenly sober again, turned to the lectern in the front of the Great Synagogue where the aged rabbi, Judah ben Gershom, had been leafing through a commentary on the Book of Esther. Rabbi Judah looked up at the stranger with his metal rod, scratched his bushy beard, and, without a word of protest, let himself be led into the coach. The congregants stared mutely at the ground as he passed by them on his way out the building.

The carriage set off, pulled by four immense black horses moving at breakneck speed. Rabbi Judah mumbled his prayers as he watched the landscape whirl by in the dark purple twilight. The coachman drove deep into the side of a mountain, past a few scattered villages with rickety huts, until he reached a stretch of road flanked by crumbling ancient marble villas and the ruins of pagan temples overgrown with weeds. Judah spied a snake slithering through a hole in an old decaying wall.

The carriage eventually reached the outer walls of a small fortress. The coachman shouted something that Rabbi Judah failed to catch, and then the gate opened. The carriage passed through and came to a stop in front of the entrance to a tower. It was now a moonless night, quiet except for the hooting owls. The coachman stepped down, rudely pulled the rabbi from his seat and shoved him toward the door to the tower.

There he was met by a squat bald man holding a candle. With his free hand, this man motioned for Rabbi Judah to follow him up the staircase. The two proceeded in silence. Rabbi Judah focused all his thoughts on prayers and supplications to the Holy One, Blessed be He, Whose rod and Whose staff had always protected His children in the holy community of Israel.

When they had climbed to the top Rabbi Judah found himself in a suite of elegant apartments. In the light of his escort's candle he could dimly make out a series of red curtains that appeared to divide the floor into different rooms, or maybe different sections of rooms. The bald man led him through a maze of these curtains until they reached a well-lit clearing with an immense bed enclosed by yet another blood red curtain. The rabbi's guide approached the foot of the bed and addressed himself to the closed curtain: Your Lordship, the Rabbi Judah ben Gershom is here, as you had requested. The man then immediately departed.

A creaky voice, in a foreign accent, moaned from behind the curtains: Rabbi, thank you kindly for answering my summons so promptly. Please, approach me closer, so that I may see the light shining forth from your eyes.

Rabbi Judah walked slowly to the side of the bed and carefully parted the curtain. Beneath a thick sumptuous blanket he saw a hideous sight: the enemy and persecutor of Israel himself, covered in sores and boils, his body shriveled, and sweat pouring steadily down his forehead.

The wicked one spoke again to Rabbi Judah: You are no doubt wondering why I have summoned you here so suddenly.

You do not need to fear for your safety. I am a Jew, and I long for the comfort of a fellow Jew as I pass from this world to the next one. Everything I have done has been for the sake of Israel and its redemption.

Words cannot describe Rabbi Judah's bafflement. He tried to formulate a response, but did not know where to begin—how to address a Haman when that Haman insists he is a holy, saintly Jew?

The wicked one continued: You are confused, I can see that. To do what was necessary for the redemption of Israel, I had to deny my Jewishness, and even do acts of unspeakable evil and violence. Yet it was all necessary to bring the world to a wondrous bliss that our puny minds, consumed by the trivial prattle of everyday nuisances, cannot imagine. I donned a mask, a perverse caricature, so that I could do the grave and terrible work needed to ensure that the Holy One, Blessed be He, should finally send his Messiah to deliver Israel from exile and the world from sin and misery.

Unfortunately, I failed in my task. My life is ebbing away now, these boils will overrun me soon. I want my family in Spain to know what became of me and to know that I devoted myself, at great peril to my soul, to the deliverance of Israel from suffering. Please, Rabbi, listen to my tale, and then write it all down in the holy tongue and send it to my relatives. They will believe you as you are a famous scholar of the Torah, even though so much of what I must say will be difficult for them to understand. Will you listen?

Rabbi Judah was now even more perplexed. But if this man was a Jew, and needed comfort and guidance on his deathbed, then it was the rabbi's obligation to assist him. Perhaps he was ready to repent for his many crimes?

So Rabbi Judah agreed to hear the wicked one's tale.

II. A Boy Dreaming of the Messiah

THE WICKED ONE began: My real name, which I have not used in many years, is Joseph della Reina. I was born in Toledo, in Spain. My father was a righteous man. He devoted himself day and night to the study of the holy books, living more in the *bet midrash* than in our family's modest apartment. I used to bring him his meals and would sit on his lap and listen to him speak of holy matters. He cared nothing for this world—a cesspool of illusions and lies he called it—and spoke always instead of the higher realms and the holy sages and the prophets. His eyes seemed never to look directly at anything or anyone, but were always wandering to a faraway point that nobody else could see.

My mother labored to support me and my brothers. She sold eggs and fruit in the marketplace, and after a day of haggling and hawking, she would come home and cook for us, cursing her worthless husband for his refusal to descend to Earth to make a living. My older brothers agreed with these reproaches wholeheartedly—and as soon as they were old enough, they apprenticed themselves to artisans in and around our courtyard. In time, they became master craftsmen, husbands, and fathers, and the wealthiest of them took in our mother when her knees ached too miserably from squatting by her stall day in and day out. Learning held no allure for my brothers, who found the marvelous tales of the patriarchs and the sages to be nothing but a childish waste of time.

But I was different. Sneers and insults may have fallen upon my father's head from our mother and our neighbors, yet when I entered the *bet midrash* all that harshness dissolved into the air and wafted away. You have no doubt heard, Rabbi, fantastic tales of the wealth of the Jews of Spain, of the mighty Jewish courtiers who advise kings and counts and live in resplendent villas with sculpted gardens and reflecting pools. There were such men, and now and then we saw them from afar. But these were not the Jews of our courtyard.

And thus my father's *bet midrash* was not a grand library presided over by a mighty scholar, or a synagogue as spacious as a Christian cathedral, but a small building, sitting at the back of an alley, smelling of dust and rotting paper. There were books strewn about everywhere—the beadle was a nearly blind, senile old man, whose job was more community charity than useful employment—and only a few flickering candles. A handful of old men, including my father, swayed and chanted over the crumbling holy books, day and night.

In that room, everything was different—it was the world made anew, made better. My father was no laughingstock here, but a revered scholar whose opinions were humbly solicited and deeply respected. Making a living did not matter to these men. This world, they told me again and again, was a deception, an illusion created by the demonic forces unleashed by Adam's terrible sin in the Garden of Eden. This brief life was only a trial of our souls before we reached the World to Come, where we would bask in the blessing and wisdom of the Holy One, Blessed be He, and learn all the secrets of the Torah in the Celestial Academy.

And there was more. The Holy One would eventually take pity upon His children in the scattered remnant of Israel, and hear their anguished cries suffering in exile. Then, at last, this hideous world of lies and deceptions would be swept away, once and for all, and the Messiah would come, conquer all evil and reign forevermore in the true, holy Jerusalem, which will descend from the upper realms to Earth. In the Messianic Age, there would be abundant food for all without the need for any labor to grow or prepare it, and we would sit in our orange groves in the Holy Land contemplating the perfection of His creation and His Torah.

To such men as these, nourishing the soul mattered far more than satisfying the filthy, degrading appetites of the body. The marketplace terrified them—so many temptations to sin and fall, the temptations of greed, the temptations of lust. The *bet midrash* was their citadel protecting them from these pollutions. They barely ate enough to keep body and soul stitched together: a bit of black bread here, a bit of hard cheese there, washed down with sour wine.

As a boy, I seized every opportunity to sit with these men, listening to them, learning from them. There seemed to be no other reality when I was in the *bet midrash* except the words they chanted and explicated, and the beautiful tales and visions they spun for me. My brothers were often sent to fetch me home.

Their eyes, so full of disgust, shattered my bliss and filled me with shame. They would not even speak to our father. But he, gentle soul that he was, would bless me and kiss me on the cheek and forehead, and tell me in a ghostly, choked whisper to go back home and bring comfort to my mother.

Eventually I, like my brothers, grew old enough to work. Against my will I was apprenticed to a cobbler, although I never made even one decent shoe. My mind would always drift away from my task. The words of the prophets and the holy sages would come to me and lift me up into a higher realm and a lovelier place. My master would sooner or later notice me staring into space instead of working and beat me harshly for being such a wastrel.

The one bright spot was the master cobbler's daughter, a little girl named Leah. She was no more than six or seven years old when I became an apprentice. Her father had no interest in her—as a daughter, she would one day require a dowry to be married off, an irritating financial liability—and her mother viewed her as a miniature servant to help with the washing and the mending. Yet Leah's soul felt an intimation of something greater, something more kind and just in the universe. Having heard that my father, however despised, was a man who devoted himself to the teachings and tales of the holy sages of blessed memory, she began to ask me, ever so hesitantly, about the Holy One, Blessed be He. Where did He live? Did He care about all people, even little girls who could not mend anything properly? If she prayed to Him, would He answer her kindly, or be angry with her like her mother was when she asked for things?

I was overjoyed to find a companion who, like me, yearned to see beyond the illusions of the cruel physical world.

I answered her questions as best I could, and told her stories, marvelous stories—of the Garden of Eden and the Tower of Babel, of Abraham, Isaac, and Jacob, of the kings of Israel and of the holy sages. She had such hopeful eyes when she listened to me, her little hand squeezing mine.

Yet even this happiness was not meant to last. Leah awoke one morning with a burning fever and a fit of vomiting, including patches of blood. Doctors were summoned, cures were tried, but to no avail. Her condition grew worse and worse. She could not leave her bed or eat or drink. The wild fire that had ignited inside her burned and dried up her body until her soul was finally released.

I can still see the child-sized coffin the burial society brought for her. There is nothing so sad as a child's coffin. A grown woman has had her chance to live, to feel some pleasure in this world and to learn wisdom. But a young girl? What had Leah's life been—cruel indifference from her father, beatings and barked orders from her mother, and then a terrible sickness while her parents muttered angrily about the cost of her doctors and medicines? And now, without the chance to know the love of a husband or to learn the commandments of the Torah, she was to be boxed up and thrown into the dirt. In a few years, no one would even remember her. She would never have a son to say *Kaddish* for her soul.

Why had the universe been so harsh to her? Why had she merited such scant kindness from the Holy One? Would it have been so awful if Leah had been permitted to live to see her wedding day?

I could no longer bear to be in the house of the master cobbler. He seemed hardly to notice his daughter's passing, while I heard her footsteps and saw those hopeful eyes everywhere I turned. But those eyes were also now accusing me: Why had I done nothing to help her, to save her? Don't ask me what I should have done, I could not tell you, yet I somehow felt so horribly guilty thinking I had failed to keep her away from the Angel of Death.

I took to walking the streets of Toledo day and night. Everywhere I saw suffering. The beggars in the alleys or on the steps of the synagogues and churches were wretched, shivering skeletons wrapped in their boils and sores, clinging pitifully to their last scraps of life. The wealthier, however, were no more fortunate in the end. They too would be struck down eventually by disease or misfortune, and deposited back into the dust, to be forgotten soon enough. Even before their final sufferings, I could see the nervous twitches in the arrogant men and elegant ladies, that terrible anxiety pulsating under their skins that one foolhardy misstep, and all their worldly splendor would disintegrate.

The master cobbler turned me out as his apprentice. My mother and my brothers were furious, and wailed and moaned about what was to become of me and was I cursed to be a burden upon them all like our father. But what did this matter, I thought, as we all were fated to fall, sooner or later, into failure, sickness, loneliness, and death. So I had slipped first, but their turns would come too.

Nevertheless, all this suffering would end—it would end when the Messiah finally came to bring redemption to the world and sweep aside illness, death, poverty and hunger. When the Messiah comes, food and wine and milk—richer and finer than anything known even to the mightiest emperor today—will burst forth from the Earth without any labor, available freely and endlessly to all. The Temple will be rebuilt and resound with songs, and every Jew will float on a cloud to his own shady orange grove in the Holy Land. The dead will rise, and all the lost, shattered loves will be repaired and reunited.

So we had but to persevere until that blessed day. Yet for how long? Why did the Holy One force us to go through this unnecessary playacting in this world of misery, when all along He knew it would vanish one day—poof!—as if it had never been?

Plagued by these thoughts, I returned to the *bet midrash* to spend each day with my father and the other sad-eyed old men, swaying over the sacred texts and dreaming of other places and times. With the help of my father and his companions, I searched feverishly for an answer to the question: When will the Messiah come? Many scholars over many centuries had written pages upon pages of speculation on this very topic. My head would swim with the different theories and calculations. So absorbed was I that I began to forget to eat or to return home to sleep. My flesh melted away, and my eyes grew cavernous in their sockets. Even my father grew alarmed at my ill health, but nothing could shake me from my single-minded pursuit.

Yet, it was all in vain. I noticed a sobering pattern in all those pages of scholarly speculation: No matter what proofs were marshaled from the holy books, every would-be prophet had computed that the Messiah would come in his very own lifetime, and every prediction had turned out to be wrong. I concluded, reluctantly, that predicting the advent of the Messiah was a fool's errand.

So where did that leave me? The Messiah would surely come, but there was no means to fathom when this miracle would occur. I could live my whole life waiting for him, in which case I would have to make the best of this diseased world in which I was trapped. Or the Messiah could arrive to-morrow, and everything would be altered beyond my wildest imaginings.

I asked myself: Should I return to the master cobbler? Who cared about learning a trade and sweating miserably for a living if the Messiah should come tomorrow and make it all irrelevant? But if he failed to come, did I have much choice but to find some means of supporting myself?

This was madness, I told myself. Why had He, Who had created everything and is unbounded in His might, cursed His children Israel to live in such a ludicrous limbo? Why not stop the suffering, instead of letting it linger?

Particularly because the Messiah already existed. Every text I read was clear: The Holy One, Blessed be He, had cre-ated the Messiah during the six days of creation. So the Messiah simply had to move from wherever he was, enter this world and fulfill his task.

Where was he? According to some sages the Messiah re-sided in a gilded castle in the World to Come. If that were true, then I had precious little chance of finding him. But the authorities were not in agreement.

One night in the *bet midrash*, as I held my head in my palms and turned these matters over in my mind, I came across an *aggadah* about Rabbi Joshua ben Levi. Rabbi Joshua, with the aid of the Prophet Elijah, had found the Messiah living among the poor at the gates of Rome, tending to his terrible lesions and wounds.

Rabbi, I see you are nodding—you must know this tale, too. See, I told you I was really a Jew.

In my despair, I pondered whether the Messiah may still be there at the gates of Rome. If he was, then perhaps I could find him and prod and persuade him into action. This sounds like lunacy, right? I see you are holding back your laughter, Rabbi. I know, looking back on myself then, that the conceit seems absurd. All these centuries the Messiah had been lurking about the slums of Rome, yet no holy sage had been able to spur him to redeem the world, and now I, who was no great scholar, was going to accomplish all this.

But imagine the unsettled state of my soul at that moment. I had nearly starved myself to a skeleton. My head pounded terribly, and everything felt airy and unreal. I could not bear to abandon my dream of the Messianic age, of the world of easy abundance and no pain, and return to a life of bitter, petty people beating and bruising one another in a mad scramble for a handful of coins.

So I resolved to go to Rome to find the Messiah.

III. To the Gates of the Eternal City

IT WAS RIGHT after Yom Kippur that I left home on my mad quest for the Messiah. I had felt the need to purify my soul through atonement before undertaking my great mission. Tears poured out of me as I begged forgiveness for every sin. I beat my head in despair that there could be sins I had forgotten, and thus I should be unable to atone for them. In the synagogue I fell to the floor in my delirium, screaming and wailing, my eyes blinded by the flood of tears. My brothers were forced to drag me home and clean me up. They pulled off my clothes and threw water over my head. Their lips were tightly shut and their arms moved violently. I lay there inert, staring at the ceiling, my mind focused on begging the Holy One, Blessed be He, for forgiveness and for another year of life to fulfill my quest.

That night, at the meal breaking the Yom Kippur fast, I ate heartily for the first time in many months. I belatedly recognized that my journey needed at least some strength of body. My newfound appetite made my mother smile—I am sure she thought I was now finally returning to my senses.

The next morning, I told my father I urgently needed to speak to him. My mother and my brothers would never comprehend my quest, but my father, who had devoted his life to higher things, would help me, I was certain. So I pulled him aside into the alley outside the *bet midrash*.

That alley lay between the high back walls of two imposing courtyards, leaving it veiled in perpetual gloom. Although he was so close I could hear his wheezing breath, my father appeared to my eyes like a spectral outline of a man. I spoke eagerly and quickly to this shadow, telling him of my plan to go to Rome to find and confront the Messiah.

My father was aghast. This is from your evil inclination, he told me. It is a terrible sin to try to hasten the end of times. He told me to trust in the Holy One, Blessed be He, Who had His own plan, which we could not hope to grasp with our limited minds. Trust Him, do not be so arrogant as to second-guess His ways. Try to elevate your soul by contemplating His endlessly wondrous Torah.

But what good is the Torah, I shot back. A set of laws to regulate humanity in a world degraded by greed, lechery, disease and violence. None of this would matter once the Messiah came. What need could there be for laws about adultery when there will be no adultery? Once the Messiah comes the urge to sin will be gone forever. Why must we be made to suffer waiting for the day when sin and misery will simply dissolve into the air, as if they had never been?

My father sighed. This talk will lead you to a bad end, he said. Then he tried a new approach. How will you travel to Rome? You have no money for carriages and inns and food. You are barely alive as is—you, a faded sack of rattling bones, cannot survive such a long journey. Your arrogance will be re-paid tenfold in hunger and disease.

It makes no difference if I live or die, I replied. If I die, I will be freed from this wretched world of pain and misery.

My father tried one last tack. Have pity on me, he said, you are the comfort of my old age. Your brothers, your mother, they look at me with such hard, unfeeling eyes. But you, my Joseph, you see the same beautiful visions I do in the sacred writings, and your eyes look with honor and esteem upon me. I doubt I have much longer in this life, and it is your presence that sweetens the bitterness of these last years.

These words did move me. I felt pity for him, as he was treated callously by his family, who should have honored his dedication to study. I hesitated. Perhaps the journey could be postponed a few years. But no—in a few years I would be forced into a trade and become responsible for the support of a wife and children.

Later that day I set out for Rome.

It was not an easy journey. I had nothing to support my-self but mad dreams and even madder despair. I traveled northward in Spain, from one Jewish community to another, begging alms from the synagogue beadles. I was often in a crowd of roving beggars, and we would be herded some-where—a poorhouse or dirty backbenches in the synagogue—where well-fed, irritated men would throw scraps of bread and rusted coins at us.

The beggars were a parade of this world's sufferings—blind men, lame men, diseased men. I asked these men how they had come upon these afflictions. Some were born this way, others had been stricken. They had clearly suffered unjustly.

Some had brought their troubles upon themselves. One beggar had once been a successful wine merchant, but had indulged repeatedly in fornication with prostitutes to the point that he became afflicted with a loathsome disease, which ate away at his body and ravaged his sanity. Once his sickness was manifest, his family and his customers abandoned him, and he lost all his wealth and all his friends.

Yet I pitied him, too. He was genuinely penitent. And why had he been cursed with such powerful lusts, with such an awesome *yetzer ha-ra*, an inclination to sin, so that he could never find peace from his itching, tormenting desires? He no doubt had felt ashamed of himself, and had not wanted those desires. They were foisted upon him somehow—by a demon perhaps? His terrible fall and sufferings were the fault of this awful world, of its myriad debased passions and temptations. In the Messianic Age, when all such sinful itches would be permanently washed away, such tragedies could never occur.

And there was the cruelty of the men who distributed the alms. We would be shunted to a corner while the synagogue beadle performed his other duties, sweating in the damp heat and making nervous chatter with each other. When the beadle finally came to do with us what the community required him to do, he had a look of such disgust in his eyes. He did not want to see us, or hear us, or smell us. We were told to eat, keep quiet and clear out in a few days' time. Needless to say, no one else in these holy communities of Israel came near us.

The other beggars asked me for my story. You appear young and able-bodied, why are you begging? Can't you earn an honest living?

In my naïveté, I told them the truth: I was going to Rome to find the Messiah to urge him to take up his holy mission now, no more delay, and to end all suffering and misery.

The beggars laughed, but it was an angry laughter. The insults flew forth from their lips: Idiot, fool, stupid boy—don't you know the Messiah is not coming? Or at least not until long after we are dead? Do you think you, some beggar Jew, are the new Moses, ready to deliver the entire human race from bondage? You are dirt, boy, a walking pile of rags and filth, a blind rodent groping in a gutter. A horse's hoof could crush your skull tomorrow and no one would care.

But if there is no Messiah, I asked them, why bother going on? Why not simply kill yourselves here and now, instead of dragging out this miserable existence?

And they had no answer for me. They struggled on because that was what they knew how to do. A couple of beggars told me they looked forward to the occasional rich man's wedding, where they could taste wine, meat and warm pastries. Yet, by and large, they looked away and stopped talking.

There was worse to come than beggars and beadles. I kept walking north, past the areas where Jews lived, and into the Pyrenees. It was winter and the hard wind smacked and beat my skin. My feet sank into the snow and my flimsy shoes, already so worn from my travels, could not keep me dry. I shivered constantly. My toes became black and numb, and the skin on my hands turned a greenish hue. With only a few stale pieces of bread left, I was sure I was going to die, either from hunger or the creeping gangrene.

Tremendous drifts of snow began to fall, and the road was soon submerged beneath the growing expanse of whiteness.

Everywhere I turned there was nothing but stiff packed snow and loud, circling winds. I was the only living thing crawling about in this stormy abyss. Something hit me in the head—hail perhaps—and knocked me over. I was sure that my end had come.

But when I looked up again, the snow in front of me had cleared away, like the Red Sea parting, and a figure was walking towards me, covered in a brown cloak and hood. This is the Angel of Death, I thought, here to take me away.

The figure came closer and bent down over me. I closed my eyes tightly, hoping the final blow from the fiery sword would be swift. Yet then, through the wind and the snow and the hail, a smell crept into my nostrils: the sweet, floral fragrance of a rich woman's perfume.

I opened my eyes and beheld a woman directly above me, although I could not see her face clearly. A few strands of blue-black hair fell over her cheek onto me. She stroked my forehead. I felt a rush of life stir within me.

She spoke to me in a soft, lilting voice: Joseph, poor, dreamy man, this is no place for you. Your task is noble, and I cannot let you die here in the wilderness without having set foot in Rome. When you wake, your wounds will be healed, and you will be on the other side of these mountains. In your hands will be a purple purse embroidered with signs and letters you cannot decipher. This is the Purse of Fortunatus. You may draw as many gold coins from it as you like, as it will never empty. Its bounty will see you safely to Rome and to the next stage of your journey.

Then she closed my eyelids with her fingertips. My body felt warm, and the ground felt as soft as a pile of silken sheets. And when I awoke, I was lying on a meadow near a town on the other side of those wretched mountains. The black and green had vanished from my skin, and in my hand was a purple purse covered in mysterious markings.

I picked myself up, and rejoiced at being healed. I clutched the purse in my hand tightly but was too nervous to open it. Soon I arrived at the gates of the town. I now had a decision to make: go begging as before or test the powers of the purse. There were all sorts of people around me entering and exiting the town—peasants hauling carts of produce, monks, an armed man or two—and it struck me how easy it would be for any of them to overpower and rob me.

So I discreetly slipped away to a large tree off the road and sat down on the far side where the wide trunk concealed me from curious glances. My hands shook as my fingers dipped into the purse for the first time. I felt nothing—not even the fabric—just empty air, a void. But then, slowly, something metallic took shape in my palm, and soon there were many of them. I pulled my hand out and—behold!—there were at least a dozen gold coins. After quickly turning my head about to make sure again that no one was watching me, I dropped these coins into the satchel where I had been keeping the meager spoils of my begging.

I stared at the purse for some time. This magic seemed to be too good to be true. Perhaps this was a test to make sure I was not consumed by greed—perhaps if I put my hand back into the purse my fingers would become frostbitten once more or there would be some other horrible punishment. But eventually curiosity conquered fear, and in went my fingers a second time. And when my fingers emerged again, they were grasping even more gold coins.

Now I knew that my quest to seek out the Messiah and hasten the redemption had the Holy One's sanction and blessing. How else could these miracles have occurred? The Holy One, Blessed be He, could have easily cut short my life in the snowdrifts in the mountains, but His emissary, in the form of a beautiful maiden, had saved me and now blessed me with whatever wealth I needed to travel to Rome on my pilgrimage.

I still needed to acquire suitable clothes. A beggar in rags throwing about gold coins will no doubt be clapped in chains as a thief. Yet the Holy One helped me again: A little way off in the distance, I spied an overturned carriage. Inside were a group of wealthy notables, young men like myself, who seemed to have died from the impact of the fall. When I approached the wreckage, I saw that there was a man lying on his side in the back who seemed to have died of a head wound, but his clothes had remained intact and unstained. I climbed into the broken carriage and carefully stripped off the clothes I needed. After washing in a nearby stream, I dressed myself according to my new status.

Now that I wore fine clothes and strode boldly with an erect bearing, crowds parted for me and eyes were respectfully lowered. I found the inn in town and paid for the most luxurious room. I explained that I was a traveling Jewish merchant and directed the innkeeper's daughter to fetch me food from the town's Jewish butcher and Jewish baker. That night my belly was finally filled, and my flesh began to fill out properly.

But there was no need to linger in that particular town. I purchased a carriage and four fine dapple grays, hired a coachman and so we set off . . . off . . .

At this point in his tale, the wicked one, Joseph della Reina, rolled over and emitted a series of horrible moans and hacking coughs. When the wicked one turned around to face him again, Rabbi Judah could see blood splattered on his chest. No doubt drawn by the terrible sounds, a retinue of the wicked one's physicians and retainers soon arrived. A heavyset man grabbed Rabbi Judah by the elbow and led him out of the room.

The pair exited the tower. There was no moon shining that night, and the clouds blocked the stars, leaving the occasional torch as the only dim light. Rabbi Judah could not tell where he was being taken, but eventually found himself inside a small villa in the same fortress complex. The heavyset man directed him to a spacious room with a canopied bed, chair and table. A torch flickered in a notch on the wall.

A young woman entered and apologized for having failed to invite the esteemed guest to dine in the great hall, but her lord had insisted on detaining the visitor for such a long time by his bed. Nevertheless, as a token of her lord's gratitude, she was delighted to present two loaves of *challah* bread and a flask of mead, both courtesy of the local Jewish baker. A note, scrawled in Yiddish, accompanied the victuals. She exited politely.

Rabbi Judah decided that the Yiddish note was sufficient proof of the kosher provenance of his meal and ate eagerly. Once his belly was full, he paced about the room. The torch light soon faded away. Despite the late hour and the darkness, he still could not sleep.

The rabbi's thoughts were a jumble. How could the wicked one, the latter day Haman, who had so persecuted the

                      Barak A. Bassman

Duchy's Jews, believe himself to be a good and righteous Jew? This man had urged the murder and dispossession of countless sons of Israel. Yet he now wished, apparently, for the rabbi's— friendship? Blessing? Understanding of his crimes? And the tale he had spun, of Messiahs and magic maidens and bottomless purses, where was this madness leading?

Or was the wicked one toying with the rabbi, lulling him into false friendship before betraying and murdering him. Or worse: torturing him until he confessed to malicious slanders against the Jews of the Duchy—enough proof, in the Duke's eyes, to eradicate once and for all, the pestilence of Israel's remnant from his lands.

Rabbi Judah decided to try to rest. The canopied bed made him uneasy: Its curtains were thick, like those in the bed of the wicked one, and the sheets smelled strongly of perfume. For what remained of the black night, the rabbi slept fitfully in the room's wooden chair. As his eyelids closed, his lips mumbled prayers to the Holy One, Blessed be He, to remember and protect His children Israel, and to give the rabbi guidance and understanding during this ordeal.

IV. Beggars and Lepers at the Gates of Rome

THE SOUNDS OF servants bustling outside his window woke the rabbi. The sun had risen and lit the room too harshly. In the bright rays of the cold morning light, the thick red curtains about the bed appeared dusty and faded. Rabbi Judah stood up slowly, and despite his stiff neck and aching knees, recited his morning prayers from memory, sad that he had been seized by the wicked one's men before having had the chance to pack his *tfillin* and *siddur*.

When he was finished, his thoughts turned back to his grim situation as a gilded prisoner in this fortress. No doubt his community, his wife and his children and his grandchildren, all feared the worst and were fervently praying for his safe return. His stomach cried out for a warm roll smeared with goose fat, but no one had bothered to attend to the hungry rabbi.

What to do now, he asked himself. Attempting escape was out of the question: An old man with gouty feet and creaking joints, he would never make it past the tightly guarded walls. Nor did it seem safe to wander about this place. Who knew what enemies of Israel roamed its precincts, with hands eager to plunge a dagger into a soft rabbinical belly.

Rabbi Judah sat down again in the chair and sighed. He looked about the room—so many thick curtains and pillows drenched in sickly sweet perfumes, but no books. It occurred to the rabbi that he had not yet seen a single book anywhere in the fortress complex. How could this wicked one, this so-called Joseph della Reina, truly be a Jew, the rabbi mused, if he could live so easily without books? Even if not the holy books of the mighty Jewish sages, may their memory be for a blessing, but at least some book, maybe some Christian version of *Aggadah* telling tales of their saints. Jewish souls need books and stories just as fish need water. This wicked one could not be a Jew.

So ran Rabbi Judah's thoughts as he stared at the floor. The bustle outside had quieted, and feeling restless, he walked to the window. The day was beautiful: sunny but crisply cool, with the wind rustling the dead leaves on the ground. A bird perched on a tree was singing a melancholy song. The rabbi recalled that King Solomon had known the language of the birds. Perhaps the wise king could have translated this bird's song. Maybe the bird was old, and maybe he now sang sadly of how his body, which once flew so easily and gracefully in the sky, throbbed with pain when he stretched his wings. Or how sad he was that his wife of many years had passed on to the World to Come, leaving him lonely in his last days. It was autumn, the season of last gasps and dissolving hopes. Maybe the bird had seen the leaves fading to orange and brown, and sang to the tree to comfort it for the loss of its once blooming foliage. Rabbi Judah almost shed a tear as he pondered the bird's unhappy plight. He mumbled a prayer to the Holy One, Blessed be He, to receive the bird's soul with love and kindness when its time would come to enter the next world.

Listening to the bird and letting his thoughts drift, the rabbi lost track of time and forgot his hunger and thirst. But eventually his reverie was interrupted by a knock at the door. In walked the same young servant girl who had attended to him the night before. She carried a tray that held a tall glass of water and a platter of bread and cheese.

Excuse me, Father, sir, she said. I do not know how to address Jewish priests properly. My Lord asked that you eat and drink now, and then he will receive you again.

She lay the tray down on the table near the chair. Please sir, sit, eat. It is more of the Jewish food we sent out for. No pork here, I swear by the Holy Virgin.

Rabbi Judah ate and drank in silence. After a time, he looked up and noticed the servant girl was still standing in the corner.

My Lord ordered me to wait until you were finished and then to take the tray from you, she said. So I have to stay here.

The rabbi nodded absently and returned to the tasks of eating and drinking. The servant girl's presence made him nervous. She was pretty and sweetly innocent. Was she a trap sent by the wicked one, to lure him into some crime that would provide a pretext to bring down new calamities upon the people of Israel? He wished she would go and glared at her to make her understand that she was not welcome. She picked up the tray as soon as he was finished and walked off quickly without further word.

Moments later a burly man, stinking of garlic and cradling a sword, entered the room. The Lord wishes to see you again, Jew, he said. Follow me.

The rabbi followed the man out of the small villa. Based upon the position of the sun, Rabbi Judah judged it to be early afternoon. The courtyard was empty except for an old woman in a corner slowly peeling potatoes with her venous fingers.

The pair walked back toward the tower where the wicked one lay in bed. As they approached the door, the wind lifted a pile of crinkled orange leaves and tossed them about. In the light of day, the rabbi could see that the short steps leading to the tower door were being dislodged by aggressive brownish weeds pushing up through the cracks in the stone.

The burly man led Rabbi Judah to the same bedroom he had visited the night before. After parting the bed curtains and announcing the rabbi's presence, he left. The wicked one motioned to the rabbi to approach him. He was well-groomed and composed, although his breathing was labored.

Rabbi Judah, I hope my servants have treated you well. You have been fed the kosher food and drink we sent for?

Yes, Lord, I have been treated with great honor and courtesy.

Good, good.

The wicked one, Joseph della Reina, paused and wheezed miserably, before launching into his tale again:

The Holy One, Blessed be He, had gifted me with the Purse of Fortunatus, so I was able to travel to Rome as a rich, distinguished man. With four horses, a gilded carriage, and a coachman who scared away the riffraff, I proceeded rapidly. My belly was filled so plentifully that I grew a respectable paunch—too many slices of honey cake—and my cheeks flapped joyfully with excess fat.

I arrived in Italy in early spring. It was like *Gan Eden*, but there were no *seraphim* with fiery swords to keep me out. The hills and fields were an explosively bright green, and the sky was endless and blue. My coachman warned me against staying in Rome itself, which he insisted was filled with thieves who would rob me blind, so I lodged at an inn in a nearby town and ordered the inn's servants to purchase kosher food for me from Rome's Jewish community.

I suspected that the Chief Rabbi of Rome would know the secret of the Messiah's location, so I was determined to pay him a visit. My first morning near Rome I ordered my coachman to draw up the horses and to enter the Jewish Quarter in grand style. I wanted to impress upon the Chief Rabbi there that I was a man to whom attention must be paid.

On the carriage ride to Rome we passed a hill upon which sat the ruins of what had once been a mighty palace. Pieces of columns and walls and floors were strewn around, some with faded frescoes of elegant men and women arguing and flirting and hunting. Idols of pagan gods with missing limbs lay about. Everything in this rubbish pile was dulled from coatings of dust—that is, except for the most startling ruin on the hill which did not appear to be a ruin at all: a gleaming white marble statue, which looked like it had just been delivered from the sculptor's studio. This statue depicted, in terrifying lifelike detail, a tall woman in an immodest dress, with her head thrown back and her long hair falling wildly over her shoulders and chest. She was looking down towards the road. I felt she was watching our carriage as we went. She struck me as so very beautiful and so strangely familiar.

Into the city we went, and we found our way to the synagogue. I sent my coachman inside to ask, in his broken Italian, for the Chief Rabbi, and to explain that his master, a Spanish Jew of vast wealth, wished for an immediate private audience. Several minutes later my coachman returned and ushered me inside.

The Chief Rabbi was a shriveled old prune with failing eyesight. He addressed me in flowery and fawning Hebrew, but my Hebrew was too poor to carry on the discussion I wanted to have. So the beadle fetched a Spanish Jew who had moved to Rome, a physician who tended to the powerful officials of the Church, to serve as our interpreter.

The Chief Rabbi asked me what had brought such a fine and noble merchant to Rome. Did I have some business with the Church or one of its orders? Perhaps a monastery had defaulted on a loan? Or was there trouble in Spain, and had I been sent to the Pope to avert an evil decree from a local prince?

I assured him there were no evil decrees to be averted. I explained I had come to find the Messiah among the beggars at the Gates of Rome, as described in the Talmud, and sought the Chief Rabbi's aid in locating him.

The physician-interpreter looked at me with disbelief as I spoke. He asked me, softly, to repeat my words again more slowly, so he could be certain to convey them accurately in Italian. After I did so, he shook his head and relayed the message.

The Chief Rabbi squinted and gave me a concerned look. He then told me that, whatever may have been the case centuries ago when the great sages of the Talmud—may their memory be a blessing—walked the land, the Messiah had long since departed from Rome.

Where had he gone, I asked.

Who knows, the Chief Rabbi answered. And who cares? The Messiah is wherever he is, which is wherever the Holy One, Blessed be He, wishes the Messiah to be. When the ordained time arrives and the redemption commences, the Messiah shall reveal himself to Israel. Until then, why should you bother the poor Messiah? Let him be. Go back to your business, raise fine sons and teach them Torah.

I was not happy with this response, so I argued back: I intend to confront the Messiah with the horrible consequences of his inexplicable delays, the unnecessary death and suffering and disease. I will demand he put an end to all this terrible pain, which is easily within his power.

The Chief Rabbi sighed, a sound like a distant, hollow whistle. Esteemed sir, I can tell from your distinguished bearing that you are no fool. So why do you speak in such a foolish manner? We cannot hasten the end. When it is the ordained time, the redemption will happen. We must be patient, and trust in the Holy One's infinite wisdom and goodness. If the Messiah was here, he would tell you the same thing. Recall that Rabbi Joshua ben Levi of blessed memory did meet the Messiah at the Gates of Rome. If it were proper, don't you believe that such a great sage would have persuaded the Messiah to commence Israel's redemption from exile and captivity?

You are just one Jew, you are not responsible for ushering in the Messianic Age all by yourself. You should rest from your journey. Perhaps you could offer some support for the poor Jews of this community? There are many aching bellies that could use the aid of a rich man like you. Or maybe you could help pay the salary for our *cheder* teacher, so the young children can continue to learn Torah. There are many important, good deeds to be done while we await the Messiah's arrival.

The Chief Rabbi's words made me suspicious. He seemed to be scheming for a large share of my wealth to use as he saw fit through the communal institutions under his and his friends' control. I was convinced now that he knew exactly where the Messiah was in this city, but was determined, out of his own base greed, to deflect me from my noble quest.

So I decided to conduct my own search. Ignoring the Chief Rabbi, I asked the physician-interpreter where I could find the beggars and lepers in the city. He refused to say, instead lecturing me from his medical knowledge, about the many dangers attendant upon mixing with such people. My patience having run out, I walked away in the middle of his speech and reentered my carriage. I instructed the coachman to find where the beggars congregate, as I wished to make a charitable contribution for their upkeep.

Asking around, we eventually found the city's most squalid section. Figures passed by slowly, groping around them, struggling with missing eyes or limbs or hideous boils leaking puss over their skin. They had formed a sprawling human horseshoe around a convent where, I surmised, alms or medicine must be distributed.

When the beggars saw my carriage, their dirty fingers rushed at me, their hoarse voices pleading for charity from the rich man. I reached into the purse, removed two huge handfuls of gold coins, and scattered them outside the carriage window. The gleeful beggars dove to the ground and fought each other for the loot. Taking advantage of their momentary distraction, I ordered my coachman to return to our inn in the countryside.

On the way back we again passed the same hill covered in ruins. My eyes turned involuntarily toward the gleaming statue of the immodestly dressed, arrogant woman. I thought I saw her marble eyes smile at me, ever so slightly.

I considered my situation. I could not explore the beggars' quarter outfitted as a rich man, but would need to conceal myself in rags. Yet then what? How to find the Messiah amidst all those wretched men? Rabbi Joshua ben Levi had been able to avail himself of the assistance of the Prophet Elijah. I could not even persuade the local Jewish physician to help me.

Still, there were certain things I knew. The Messiah would be a Jew. So I needed to find a Jewish beggar. One who gave off some radiance beneath his sores and lesions and tattered robes.

After procuring suitable rags and rubbing dirt into my cheeks and fingernails, I spent several days wandering among the beggars. In the beginning I could find no other Jews and was spit upon by the Roman beggars as a filthy Christ killer who did not deserve the holy sisters' kind charity.

Yet, once I found the little colony of Jewish beggars, none of them shined with any radiance. These men debated whether to pretend to be Christian to take advantage of the nuns' benevolence and apparently excellent cooking. One beggar in particular I recall, who was missing an arm, explained that he supported himself by traveling about Europe pretending to convert. He would find a local monastery or pious noble house and regale them excitedly with accounts of a dream in which the truth of Christianity had been revealed to him. Jubilant at the news of a Jew seeing the truth of their religion, the Christians would give him comfortable lodging and ample food as they prepared for his conversion. But always on the morning he was to be baptized, he would run away. Thus, in his depraved mind, he had remained a good and loyal Jew, even if he was forced by circumstances to eat unclean, albeit sumptuous, gentile delicacies.

The evening after meeting these Jewish beggars I sat alone in my room in the inn and stared at the wooden beams in the ceiling. I could not understand what was happening to me. I had been miraculously saved from death in the snow drifts by mysterious powers, who had also bestowed unlimited wealth upon me. There must have been some purpose behind these extraordinary acts—why would an angel rescue me and hand me a magic purse so I could travel to Rome and accomplish nothing? This could not be the end of my quest. Something else was lurking nearby, something wondrous, but what?

The sun slowly sank and my room faded into a thick darkness that now hid the bumps and crevices in the old ceiling. It is late, I told myself, close your eyes and let sleep carry you away from your troubles. Yet I could not sleep.

I stepped over to the window. On a distant hill there was light—but not moonlight, these were candles or torches, sending bright orange flames up into the night sky. There was a faint hum drifting down from the hill, as if many people were chattering away at an outdoor banquet.

I dressed, went downstairs and stepped outside. The clouds above my head then parted suddenly, revealing the moon's soft white light, and the road that ran past the inn became visible once more. I strode onto the wobbly cobblestones and walked toward the hill with the orange lights, from whence I could hear even more clearly the sounds of the revelries.

As I went along, the happy, raucous voices grew louder and closer. I turned off the road and went up towards the brilliantly lit hill. Nearing the top, a meadow with a pavilion came into view, filled with masked partiers—like at carnival in Italy—clinking glasses of wine. A man, as big as an oak tree, wrapped in a crimson hauberk and carrying a long sword, approached and told me to halt.

Let me see your arms, he said to me in Spanish. In my trancelike state, I did not question why this guard spoke Spanish and how he had known to use the language with me.

I mutely obeyed.

My arms were now covered in purple circles, the color of the magic Purse of Fortunatus. The giant smiled when he saw these markings.

Pull your sleeves back down, good sir, you are a welcome reveler at this fine masked ball.

And he bowed, stood aside, and pointed me forward.

Into the crowd I floated, although I was the only guest who had not donned a carnival mask. I could not understand the revelers' rapid Italian conversations. Wild, hideous masks moved about me—long, curving noses, intensely colored grinning jesters with tinkling bells, men with two sorrowful golden faces on their heads. I barely kept my balance, yet somehow the masked revelers danced and weaved about me so that we never collided. A drink was placed into my hand, a too sweet, overripe red wine. I drank it to the dregs in one gulp.

The voices around me grew louder, yet I still could not make out what they were saying. Music played, also loud, too loud for me. I felt hot, my head pounded, my glass slipped from my hand, my feet wavered, and down I fell.

When I opened my eyes a few minutes later, I could hear the revelers nearby, but I was somewhere else now, lying on a stone slab. Pulling myself up, I could see I was in an elegant garden. There were statues of pagan gods, idols, neatly placed in a circle around an artificial pond. Within this pond was a fountain bubbling in a steady, low rhythm. Behind the statues were flower beds and then high stone walls covered in criss-crossing vines. I went to the water, bent down, and smelled its fresh honeyed scent. With my finger I tasted a little.

I heard someone walking toward me. When I turned around I saw a woman, tall and slender, wearing a white expressionless mask that covered her face and outlined her lips and eyes in turquoise. On top of her head was piled a huge bulk of black hair in a tightly woven and many-pinned bun.

I think the festivities were too much for you, she said to me in Spanish. I would like to show you my gardens.

Her voice was gentle and familiar, but I could not recall who she was.

Come with me, she said.

And she took my hand and led me through a door in the far garden wall that led to another pavilion overlooking the dark, sleeping countryside. Inside that second pavilion were two marble chairs, but otherwise the structure was empty. We each sat in one of the chairs.

Joseph, you look so sad, she said. Unburden your heart.

How do you know my name? I asked.

Have you already forgotten me, so soon? We met in the mountains, on the snowdrifts. Those are my purple love bites on your arm.

Now I recalled that voice: It was the angel who had healed my body, spirited me away from danger and showered me with boundless wealth.

I see from your eyes that now you do recognize me, Joseph.

I asked her to remove the mask so I could see her face.

No, not tonight, she said. Do not trouble yourself about the mask. But tell me, what makes you sigh so pitifully? You have made it to Rome, and as a wealthy man. You have what you wanted.

No! No, I do not! I screamed these words at her. As my voice rose, so did the revelers' riotous cackling in the distance.

I came, I continued, to find the Messiah among the beggars at the Gates of Rome, to confront him about his cowardly refusal to step forward and redeem the world from suffering. But he is nowhere to be found. It was all in vain.

You have done nothing in vain, the masked lady replied. You were saved for a reason—there are hidden forces, powerful spirits. They have great expectations for you. If you would like we can visit the Messiah now. I know where he rests at night, and he is a light sleeper.

I was so stunned at these words, uttered so matter-of-factly, that I could not mold my racing thoughts into coherent words.

But you need a mask, she continued. Real human faces can unnerve him, especially at night. He often hides from them, which is no doubt why you had so much trouble tracking him down. Here—and she reached behind her chair—put this on.

It was a pale, expressionless mask that covered my whole face. Around the lips, eyes, and cheeks were tiny purple circles, like blotches or sores. Once the mask was securely in place, she took my hand again, and we left the pavilion. We were suddenly next to the road, with a cavernous black carriage waiting. We entered, and the carriage departed without the masked lady telling her coachman where to go.

We rode in silence, holding hands. Her skin was soft, and her touch sent tremors of desire through me. I breathed hard, and tried to remain focused on my task: forcing the redemption, confronting the so-called savior who refused to use his divine gifts to blot out suffering, disease and sin.

We drove around the edge of the city until we descended down what appeared to be a steep ditch, although everything was so dark I could not tell exactly. Soon something behind us—a hill, a mound—blocked the city from our sight. The carriage eventually reached level ground again. I saw then, ahead of us, a light shining from the window of a small house sitting in the middle of an otherwise desolate meadow.

We stopped at the threshold of this house. The masked lady rapped on the door a few times. Eventually, a wheezing, stooped man opened up and invited us in. This man painstakingly sat down in his wooden rocking chair and asked us how we had happened on his out of the way hut so late in the night.

The masked lady walked over to him and looked down upon his pockmarked face.

Do not play games with me, she said, I know who you are and you know who I am. My friend, a fine Spanish Jew, has been seeking you. Reveal who you really are.

He dramatically sighed until his sigh turned into a hacking cough. Then he spoke in a faltering whisper: I am the Messiah, destined to commence the redemption and to end Israel's long suffering in wretched exile.

The masked lady continued: And why have you not begun your mission? What are you doing wasting away in this hovel?

He whispered again: It is not yet time.

The masked lady turned to me. I was seized with terror. Here he was, at last, the Messiah, and I could not speak. My hands reached to remove my mask until the masked lady hissed at me, Be still.

She turned back to the Messiah: Tell me, when will be the time?

He responded that only the Holy One, Blessed be He, knew the precise time but that it would be when the world had sunk to such an abysmal level of wickedness that it could not be permitted to endure—when the Jews will be so oppressed and downtrodden that, as after the four hundred years of bondage in Egypt, they will be forced to cry out for a new Moses, a new redeemer to lead them from slavery to freedom.

The masked lady continued: But are you not troubled by all of the suffering in the world? Why not bring it to an end now? Why must we wait?

It is not yet time, it is not yet time. Over and over he repeated that same phrase.

I began to have trouble breathing—the mask seemed to be tightening its grip on my face. I cried out in pain. The lady only laughed in response. I gagged, and she laughed harder. Soon my eyes saw nothing but darkness. I lost consciousness as my legs crumbled beneath me, and my head hit something blunt and hard.

When I awoke I was back in my bed at the inn, and the sun shone brightly into my window. The wind brought me a lovely smell of whatever flower grew wild in that part of Italy. I felt my face—no mask.

I stood up and saw something on the table in my room, on top of my magical purse. It was a carnival mask, pale and expressionless and dotted with purple circles, like the one that had attacked my face the previous night. I dared not touch it, but carefully pulled out the purse from underneath and left the demonic talisman on the table. I hoped one of the servants would steal it.

After breakfast I went for a walk to the hill where I had attended the masked ball. But the beautiful gardens were gone. It was all rubble, broken bits of some ancient idol-worshipper's pleasure villa, except for that one intact gleaming white marble statue that I had seen before from my carriage window. Its eyes seemed to be watching me. As I approached the statue I choked on the air: It was her, the masked lady, perfectly rendered by the artist. Her face was the face of the mask, and from her head tumbled long, thick tresses over her shoulders. The dress was the same, wound snugly around the same voluptuous figure. All alone with the statue on the hill of ruins, in the quiet sun-drenched morning, my heart was moved by her great beauty. I recalled how she had held my hand in the carriage, and I reached out and touched the statue's hand. While cold at first, it seemed to grow warmer as it recognized my touch. Seized with a sudden, insatiable longing, I kissed the statue's lips passionately. Regaining my senses, I was relieved that there had been no one about to witness my strange behavior.

Deciding it was best to get away from the bewitching statue, I walked farther, trying to find the Messiah's hovel. But it was nowhere to be seen. I ran myself ragged with hunger and thirst searching until, towards the late afternoon, I re-entered the city of Rome's Jewish quarter and found the old synagogue once more. The beadle recognized me, fetched me wine and cakes and summoned the rabbi and the Spanish physician.

All of them were overjoyed to see me. They were certain I had finally abandoned my lunatic scheme to find the Messiah and had decided instead, sensibly, to aid their community with my charity. They did not quite say this, but I could read these thoughts from their expressions.

The Chief Rabbi renewed his welcome to me and asked how my stay in Rome had been.

I relayed my adventures at the masked ball with the masked lady and with the Messiah. What did they make of these strange events?

The physician insisted I had some kind of illness or mental fever brought on by something foul in my blood or my diet, and what I now needed was rest and plain food. The rabbi was more concerned. Beware of old ruins, he told me, there are too many wicked ancient souls floating about these hills, demons who had haunted and tempted the idolatrous Romans of old. You should leave your inn and come stay with me. I can ward them off. Shaken as I was, I promised to consider his offer.

That night I was determined to travel to the rabbi's home. I was organizing my belongings when the innkeeper came to my door.

Pardon me, Sir, he said, but there is a carriage waiting for you out front.

I went downstairs and peeked into the elegant but pitch-black carriage parked in front of the inn's porch. Is anyone in here? I asked.

A purple light glowed, though I did not see any candle burning. And there sat my masked lady.

I tried to leave, but she drew me in with her powerful hands. It was clear that she was some sort of messenger or guide from the higher realms, as no human woman could have possessed such extraordinary strength.

Do not fear, she said. I did not save you from death and shower you with riches only to strangle you in my carriage. We are going for a ride, not to anywhere in particular, just in a loop around the hills. I want to hear how your quest is proceeding.

The carriage took off at a brisk pace. I could not see outside the opaque windows or even what was in front of me. The masked lady, who was the only thing visible in the purple light, took my hands in hers, squeezed them tenderly and urged me to unburden my troubled soul.

I told her of my despair. What, I asked, had been the point of saving me and bringing me here? Was it only so I could see the Messiah's cruel indifference with my own eyes? Was the Throne of Glory toying with me and laughing at me? The redemption must wait until there should arise a generation that is wholly wicked and Israel's oppression in exile becomes too unbearable—a generation as awful as that which preceded the

Flood—yet the world was far from sinking so low. My fellow Jews in Spain—like my own brothers—lived prosperous, peaceful lives and enjoyed decent, if not always warm, relations with their Christian and Muslim neighbors. This hideous, mediocre world, with its petty sufferings and illness and death, would stumble on, because it was not quite dismal enough to be worth the bother of redemption.

She sighed and stroked my cheek. Dear Joseph, you are too good and righteous for this world. You were spared so you could learn the truth from the Messiah's own lips. But now you must choose: What will you do with your knowledge? If you like, you can take as much money as you can carry from the purse, abandon your quest and return home. You can live comfortably, marry well and, in the years before you fall prey to sickness and death, have the pleasures of a Jewish householder. Or you may continue your quest to hasten the end of days and the redemption of mankind from every kind of misery.

Continue—but how? I asked. How can I bring about the redemption?

How indeed, she replied. You know the truth now. So, how indeed?

And then I saw the harsh truth: The world was cursed not because of the truly wicked or the truly righteous, but rather because of the officious, bumbling mass of people in between. All those decent Jews and their decent neighbors plodding ahead, not terribly saintly but not terribly sinful either. They kept the world from spiraling into the abyss of wretchedness that alone could bring true redemption and end all suffering and death.

You, Rabbi Judah, you and your ilk are the greatest enemies of Israel. With your good-enough-for-now guidance, you prop up this horrible world and stop it from slipping into the cesspool of evil and slaughter that alone will force the end. Your actions prevent the Messiah from coming, and so you and those like you are responsible for all the sickness and death and suffering in the world. You are a murderer, many, many times a murderer!

The wicked one, Joseph della Reina, shouted these words and pointed a forefinger, ravaged with peeling dry sores, at Rabbi Judah's heart. Rabbi Judah forced himself to be still and silently offered desperate pleas to the Holy One, Blessed be He, to see him safely through this horrible trial.

The wicked one rasped wretchedly, and a sore on his right cheek burst, releasing pus down the side of his face. Tears had fallen from his eyes. Yet a moment later, the wicked one had composed himself again.

My apologies. You are my guest, here to learn the truth from my lips, and that was a rude and unfortunate outburst. So my sincere and humble apologies.

What had I been saying? The carriage ride, the purple light . . . yes . . . my epiphany. So, like just now, I then blurted out this discovery in the carriage at the top of my lungs.

The masked lady did not flinch. Of course, I had no idea what her expression was beneath that mask, but the calmness in her limbs convinced me she was not surprised or upset at my outburst. She simply replied, in a gentle tone: What then will you do about this problem? How shall my dear Joseph della Reina continue his quest?

I was silent for a long time. The truth was before me, quite clear, but I retreated from it. The only way to bring about the redemption was to engineer the world's fall into the unspeakable state of evil that must precede it. To save the people of Israel, I would need to raise their torments to an unbearable pitch. How could I do such a thing? Could I steel myself to cause so much suffering, even if I knew it was ultimately for the sake of everyone's redemption and—eventually—endless bliss?

The masked lady broke the silence. You know what you need to do to continue your quest. I see it in your eyes. If you choose to continue, I advise you to take baptism. That, and your boundless purse, will permit you ready access to the courts of the great nobles of Christian Europe. You have three days to make up your mind. If you have not been baptized in three days, then the Purse of Fortunatus shall vanish from your hands and return to mine, although between now and then you may withdraw as much money as you like, to use howsoever you choose, for your quest or not.

Oh, and about your mask. It was foolish of you to try to part from it. Do not worry, it is safe. If you are baptized, it will return to you. Keep it this time and watch over it. When you need to summon me in the future, simply put the mask on.

Farewell for now.

And with that, the carriage door opened, she pushed me out and I stood before my inn again. When I turned around the carriage had already disappeared.

Rabbi Judah, you of course know the choice I made. It is why we are here in this place, and why I must explain these things to you. I realized that I had been chosen for this sacred and terrible task—this other-worldly help and guidance, these magic talismans must have been from the Holy One, Blessed be He. I did not wait the full three days. The next morning, I was baptized.

The wicked one, Joseph della Reina, coughed miserably again. His body shook as if it were stranded again in the frozen snow banks of a distant mountain peak.

I must rest again. Until tomorrow, my honored guest, goodbye and enjoy my hospitality.

Rabbi Judah exited the room and informed the guard that His Lordship had asked for an opportunity to repose.

V. Into the Abyss

DESPITE THE SOOTHING quiet of the calm night, Rabbi Judah could not sleep. The wicked one is mad, the rabbi told himself. This is no trap—he could have murdered me long ago if that was his intention. No, he believes the truth of all that he utters. Perhaps these events unfolded as he has told me?

If they did, though, what had he truly seen? This lady and this so-called Messiah, they could not be messengers from the Holy One, Blessed be He. How could He, who loves His children Israel and shed so many tears when their many sins led twice to the destruction of His glorious Temple in Jerusalem, how could He lure a pious Jewish boy to apostasy in order to engineer even greater persecution and suffering? This wicked one had been deluded by the dark powers, the deceivers, who haunt and tempt men. But the young Joseph della Reina had been no sinner. To the contrary, his excessive faith had made him yearn for the impossible. So why had he been so mercilessly tricked and manipulated by demons?

The sun began to rise at the edge of the horizon. The fortress came gradually back to life as the servants and guards yawned, greeted each other and set about their morning tasks. The autumn leaves were a dull red and gold in the morning light. There was a comforting rhythmic crunching sound as the servants and guards trampled dead leaves underfoot into smaller and smaller bits of rubbish.

The same sweetly demure serving girl came with the rabbi's breakfast. He asked her to stay while he ate.

Girl, what is your name and where are you from?

It is Gretchen. I grew up not far from here. My parents work the lands of our Lord. They had too many daughters to feed and clothe, and my Lord kindly took me into his service. He has always been so very kind to us.

Do you know anything about Jews? Are they good people or bad people?

I don't know very much about anything, sir, I just try to serve as best I can and trust in my Savior and His Holy Virgin Mother to look after my poor, sinful soul.

At these words she grasped a small, plain wooden cross hanging down from her neck.

What would make you happy?

She looked down and brushed some loose strands of hair behind her ear. After a moment she said, with careful and deliberate enunciation, that she hoped to serve her Lord well and to obey God, and maybe someday to wed and to have a family of her own. She had repeatedly promised the Holy Virgin Mother in her prayers that she would be a good mother.

Rabbi Judah nodded absently. I am finished, he said, you may go now.

And so the girl left. He found comfort in her words. It was a relief to know that, in the madman's citadel, there were still hearts yearning merely for the blessings of a baby to swaddle and a helpmeet to lean upon. He sat down in the room's chair and stared out the window at the increasingly intense bustle of activity in the courtyard, until weariness finally overwhelmed his strained eyes and sleep claimed his body.

VI. Corruptions & Libels

THE GUARD ROUGHLY shook Rabbi Judah until he awoke, although the rabbi still felt sunk in the distant haze of drowsiness and his knees needed all their might to force his body up. After washing and drinking a glass of water that had been discreetly left for him, the rabbi silently followed the guard back to the fortress's tower, up the stairs, and into the dimly lit bedroom of the wicked one, Joseph della Reina.

That foul man's condition had deteriorated. His skin seemed to be melting away, revealing the outline of a pile of jagged bones—and what remained of that skin was covered in purplish sores and streaks of dried pus. Yet when he saw the rabbi enter, the dying lord of the tower pulled himself up against his pillow and smiled warmly.

It is good to see you again, Rabbi Judah.

His voice was hoarse, but clear.

We have reached the most difficult part of my tale, the events which no doubt will most upset my family, when I had to take bold action to try to hasten the coming of the Messiah.

These were events you have seen with your eyes and heard with your ears, but you saw and heard without understanding the deeper, true meaning. But I will tell you now.

After I had converted to Christianity, I knew I could not return home. I lingered in and around Rome, looking for a way to achieve my goal of forcing the end, the redemption. It occurred to me that, if I could gain power and influence in one principality, I could perhaps set events and ideas in motion, which in turn would spread like an evil plague from nation to nation, and eventually bring the world to such a state of wretchedness that the Messiah would be compelled to commence his mission.

The Holy One, Blessed be He, soon brought me into contact with the Duke of W., our current prince and ruler, may he live long and in good health. The Duke and Duchess were making a pilgrimage to the Holy See, accompanied by the bulk of their court. Among the traveling dignitaries was Count Otto. This Otto was—is—hardly a pious man. Bored by the devout proceedings, he had sought out and found Rome's secret gambling dens in moldy tavern basements, where he drank with abandon and lost most of his fortune in games of chance.

I met Otto one night as I was strolling near my inn outside the city. He had fled his creditors, and I found him drunk under a tree, moaning for his Creator to strike him dead with a lightning bolt, thereby ending his troubles.

Despite his wretched state at that moment, I quickly realized from his elegant garments that he was of noble birth. I helped Otto to stand up, led him back to my inn and, over jugs of wine, heard his tale of boredom and dissipation. I, on the other hand, had usefully passed my time in Rome in the study of languages, including the German that Otto spoke. I told him I believed I could be of help, but we should speak further in the morning. I paid the innkeeper to look after him that night.

The next morning Otto had breakfast with me in my room. I explained that I was a wealthy Jew, heir to a vast Spanish fortune, but, while traveling to Rome on business, I had seen the truth of the Christian religion and been baptized. Now, I continued, I was in a quandary: I could not return to my Jewish family in Spain, but I had nowhere else to start my new life as a Christian. If Otto could introduce me at the Duke's court, I would be happy, I told him, to take care of all of his debts. I could even lend additional funds to help support him until his return to his estates in the Duchy of W.

Otto laughed bitterly, and then told me the exact amount of his debts, no doubt sure I would be stunned into withdrawing my offer of aid. I merely shrugged and told him to send word to his creditors to see me at my inn to settle his accounts. And so Otto was saved from ruin by the inexhaustible Purse of Fortunatus. To his delight, I even replenished Otto's funds to the point that he had never been more flush with gold. I told him not to worry about repayment—whenever circumstances permitted, would be just fine, and there would be no interest charged on my loans.

The grateful Count Otto introduced me to the Duke, the Duchess and their court. The devout Duchess was especially moved by my plight as a Jew who had seen the truth of her faith and could not safely return to his family of nonbelievers. She agreed to accept me as her ward. Soon I was staying with the ducal family at their rented villa in Rome.

Even more useful were Otto's whispers that I was a man of extraordinary wealth and generosity. Courtier after courtier made discreet approaches—this one needed money for a dowry for his niece, that one's lands had a poor harvest and he was short of funds, another had been robbed by his servant— on and on they prattled and needled and begged. And I satisfied them all, every one, and gave even more than what was asked.

I became conscious of wielding great power. While the courtiers went through the forms of obeisance to their Duke, there was no fear or worry in their eyes as they faced him. But when they saw me, keeper of their secrets and savior of their fortunes, they trembled. There was a twitching, stuttering humility when these courtiers spoke to me. I delighted in this new sensation of being feared.

The court eventually began its return journey to the Duchy of W. in Germany. I, naturally, went along too. As we traveled north, we stopped in Venice, where the Duke had business affairs to address. Having heard of my monetary acumen, he asked me to assist him. The Duchess and the ladies of the court proceeded home.

The affair with the Venetians was protracted, as the parties had years of tangled dealings to sort through. So we were delayed in Venice.

This delay was not conducive to the Duke's virtue. With the Duchess far away, the Duke took to melancholy strolls under the moonlight in the squares and the alleys. A proprietor of a house of ill repute noticed the restless, solitary lord pacing away his sleepless nights, and, with words of false friendship and reassurance, lured the Duke into his establishment for glasses of strong wine. From there, the sight of the women of the house in alluring garments in the dim candlelight was too much for the lonely prince.

The Duke indulged more and more, with many different women, unable to resist the Devil's trap. That is, until the pustules started to spread over his body. The Duke had been stricken with the great pox—a fitting punishment for those who would defile themselves in such filthy lusts. His panic was terrible. The Duke fasted and locked himself in his private chapel, where he prayed feverishly. He sent out for whips, and took to flagellating himself to the point of unconsciousness. The Duke would not speak to anyone. When his terrified and bewildered courtiers addressed him, he seemed to look right through them, as if they were fluttering curtains, beyond which he saw the silhouette of some nightmarish vision that made him tremble and sweat.

Securing no help from his penitence, and not certain where else to turn, he confided in me—perhaps through my Spanish connections I knew of a remedy or a physician of great skill? I said I was sure I could find a cure and that all would be well for him. But I instructed him to continue to stay away from that wretched place and focus on prayer and fasting until I could find what I needed.

That night, alone in my bed chamber in the palazzo the Duke had rented, I opened a black velvet box. It had been delivered to me on the morning after my baptism, although no one could tell me who had sent it. Still, I had known immediately what it was, however much I shuddered to see the thing. But this crisis had no other solution, so I opened the box, removed the carnival mask that was inside, and placed it upon my face.

And there appeared the masked lady again, in a tightly fitted black silk dress with her black hair falling loosely over her shoulders and back.

So we faced each other, two expressionless masks. She walked in a circle about me. My dread grew—perhaps I had done something that was unwise, perhaps I had summoned a different creature than my former protector.

Finally, she spoke in a whisper: You have done well, dear Joseph. You are well along on your quest. You are almost in a position to set events in motion, which will hasten the redemption of wretched Israel in exile. As you have done so well on your own, why are you summoning me in the middle of this dark night?

That blank, pitiless mask of hers, so deathly white, bore into me, and for a moment I lost my power of speech. I eventually found my bearings again and spoke, also in a whisper: The Duke, alone here without the Duchess, has fallen into terrible sin and contracted a loathsome disease, the great pox. He needs a cure—if I can procure it for him . . .

My words trailed off. Silently, the masked lady held her hand up level to my eyes. She clenched her fist, moaned and then unclenched it, revealing a small red vial, which she placed on the table by my bed. I looked over at the bottle, which emitted a sweet burnt odor, but when I turned around again she had vanished.

The next morning, I visited the Duke in private. Drink the contents of this red vial, my Lord, I said, and all will be well.

Do not ask what I needed to do to find this cure. Thank our merciful Savior and drink it to the dregs.

By evening, the loathsome pox had withered away, the pustules had healed and the Duke was cured. We never spoke again about this incident. But afterwards, His Excellency showed me special regard. Anyone who failed to honor me was harshly rebuked and sometimes beaten. The court soon understood that to say a spiteful word against me was to guarantee a fall from favor. The Duke showered me with titles and estates—this one we are in now among them—and many times he sought my counsel.

After this near disaster involving the good prince's morals and health, he was eager to return home. I was asked to procure whatever sums were necessary to buy the acquiescence of the Venetian merchants to settle all outstanding disputes. Reaching into the Purse of Fortunatus, this was easily accomplished. The Duke asked me for an accounting of the sums spent, but I said it was an honor to aid a Christian prince who had the kindness and mercy to take a lonely, outcast Jewish convert into his household, and this was simply my modest attempt at conveying my gratitude.

The court soon returned to the Duchy of W. I was installed in a suite of apartments in a high tower in the Duke's castle. I settled into life as a courtier and became banker to the lords and ladies of the Duchy. Count Otto once more spread rumors that the baptized Jew possessed fabulous wealth and great discretion and generosity. Even more so now, they came to me for aid and succor. This one needed money to buy the silence of the girl impregnated by his foolish son, another had overspent on banquets and hunting expeditions, or a lady bitterly resented her brutal, cheating husband and sought funds for an assassin or poison. I helped every one of them, and all those secrets slept soundly in my breast. Wherever I went, I found myself greeted by mouths brimming with words of glorious praise and by eyes trembling with terror at all that I knew.

I sometimes liked to stroll in the gardens near the castle. There, under an immense spreading beech tree, I one day beheld a white marble statue of a woman. Her pose was flirtatious—she was tilting her hips to the side and letting her hair fall over her chest. The statue had been sculpted with remarkable fidelity to the contours of a real human body. Yet it was the face that held me transfixed. It was blank and expressionless, but somehow those pale empty eyes seemed to stare intensely into me.

Evidently some enterprising soul must have noticed me gaping at the sculpture because that night I found it placed next to my bed. My servant—for a manservant had been assigned to look after my needs—explained that it was a gift from the Duke in appreciation for my fine contributions to the welfare of the Duchy. I fell asleep looking upon that blank face with a mixture of lightly floating emotions—longing, curiosity and a strange, wistful sadness.

At the midnight hour I was awoken by the sound of something stirring in my room. In the moonlight I could see the statue was gone. Someone was in my bed—she smelled of sweet perfume—her soft, firm hands removed my bed clothes. I shuddered and closed my eyes. She took me in hand and made me her lover.

When it was over I felt thick silken locks of hair brush against my chest. Overcome with pleasure and fright, I opened my eyes. There, above me, was the masked lady. She pressed her finger on my lips until I fell asleep once more. When I awoke the next morning she had vanished but the marble statue had returned to its place.

I felt uneasy, because I could not be sure if the phantom had been my protector or an evil spirit that had cunningly impersonated her to gain my trust. After all, I had never seen her face, just that blank pale mask.

I asked my manservant to move the statue away, anywhere, just far away. He did so promptly. Yet when evening fell again, it had somehow returned to the foot of my bed. Once or twice more I tried to rid myself of the thing, but it always returned. Some nights it came to life again, appearing as my masked lady and compelled me to be her lover, in a jumble of the sweetest desire and the gravest terror.

I could bear the uncertainty no longer. One evening, when the moon shone clearly, I stood in a corner facing the statue. I placed my carnival mask upon my face to summon my protector and guardian. Immediately the statue moved, the hair and dress blackened, the face became a carnival mask. It is you, I said, and not some cursed ghoul?

It is I, she said. Enjoy the favors bestowed upon you by greater powers, and do not squirm like a pitiful boy. Have the courage to delight in the pleasures granted to your flesh, before it withers away with rot and decay. You will be tested again in your quest, soon, but for now, savor the enchantments of love.

And we were lovers again, but this time without me cowering in craven, flinching fear—no, now boldly, as a man basking in his labor under the glorious sun. She visited me often after that night, and I fell deeply, passionately, in love with her. After these rapturous nights, my exhausted body would only rise with difficulty late in the morning, and I walked about in a stupor. Those who spoke to me had to repeat their words many times as I drifted along in my satisfied haze.

The love of this angel or phantom was so wondrous that I was never tempted by a flesh and blood woman again and had no desire to take a wife. The ladies of the court, trying so hard to artfully conceal the ageing of their wrinkling bodies, filled me with pity but left me empty of desire.

I wanted to know more about my lover. Who are you? I asked. Do you have a name? What kind of creature are you? Take off that mask, let me see your face, I begged her, let me taste your lips.

But she refused, always. My questions were met with silence and the blankly staring mask.

I grew to hate that mask. It hid my beloved from me. If I was to be hers and she was to be mine, I had to see her, to see her truly. Once I attempted to pull the mask off by force. My hand caught on fire, while she remained calm and still, staring with those blank white mask eyes. When I was about to faint from the unbearable pain of my flesh burning she snapped her fingers and the flame disappeared. My hand was as if it had never been harmed. I breathed hard as I gingerly flexed my fingers and felt my palm, still not believing that my hand had been restored intact to me. She stayed silent throughout this ordeal.

Suffice it to say, I never attempted to remove her mask again.

One night she told me she would have to go away and admonished me to remember my quest. She said to me: You will soon be presented with the opportunity to set events in motion that will force the Messiah to come forth to redeem all Israel from its suffering and exile. The many gifts that have been granted to you have been for this very purpose. Be brave enough and strong enough to do the dreadful acts that must be done.

The next morning the statue was gone and I could not find it anywhere. I was distraught for days pining for the touch of my otherworldly lover. But then, a tragedy in a nearby village gave me the opportunity to work once again towards Israel's redemption. Two Christian boys, each no more than eight years old, had been found dead by a creek, their blonde rosy bodies hacked and mangled.

At long last, this was my chance. I knew that if this incident could rouse the Christian population against the Jews somehow, then the sufferings of Israel could perhaps reach such a fever pitch that the Messiah would be forced to act.

Although the Duke had appointed a commission of magistrates to investigate, I demanded access to the bodies. Given my unique standing in the court, no one resisted what they must have considered a harmless, if eccentric, request. After inspecting the corpses, I announced to the Duke and the magistrates that this had to be a case of Jewish ritual murder—these boys were murdered, I insisted, so wicked Jews could use their blood to make matzo for dark and horrible secret Passover rites.

I claimed to have seen telltale markings on the bodies, punctures and wounds that showed the use of specialized Jewish implements to drain the blood and to attempt to make the deed appear to be an ordinary crime. I told them I had seen such crimes and methods with my own eyes as a Jewish boy in

Spain, where I had been forced to eat the blood-soaked matzo by my father. It was guilt and remorse for these unspeakable crimes, for the innocent Christian blood spilt, which had forced me to repent and to seek salvation from the Church.

The Duke recoiled in horror at my words. He had heard of such slanders in other countries, but not his own. Until then, he had thought his Jews loyal and honest subjects, if perhaps misguided in matters of faith.

I had assumed there would be little resistance to my libel, but Bishop Conrad, the most senior representative of the Church in the Duchy, opposed me passionately. He pointed out that the Emperor Frederick II had appointed a commission to study accusations of Jewish ritual murder, which had found them to be baseless calumnies. Pope Innocent IV and Pope Gregory X had likewise both roundly condemned such libels against the Jews. The Bishop himself had a dear friend, a most pious and learned Dominican monk, who had been born and raised a Jew before embracing the true faith. This monk had clearly explained to the good bishop the absurdity of the blood libel—Jews would not eat meat unless the blood were drained fully, nor would they eat an egg with the tiniest speck of blood on it. The notion that Jews murdered anyone to consume their blood, Bishop Conrad concluded, was simply nonsense. And if I were willing to toss about such accusations, then either I had lied about my Jewish origins or I was possessed of such a deep hatred against my former brethren that I had lost my rational faculties.

The Duke did not know what to do. The Bishop's arguments appeared to persuade him, but he was at a loss as to why I would lie, especially about a matter which, as a former Jew, I should know so well. His Excellency summoned the leaders of the Jews of the Duchy—were you among them Rabbi Judah? I cannot recall any longer—but I was not permitted to attend his discussion with them.

The Duke was soon satisfied that my ritual murder charges were unfounded slanders. We were now speaking less, and I found myself excluded from councils of state. Whispers abounded that my fall was imminent, and both the Church and the Jews pressed for my removal. Still, the Duke did not act openly against me, and I remained not only at liberty, but a well-fed ennobled guest in the same spacious suite of castle apartments.

This uneasy situation continued for several weeks. I learned later that Count Otto had led a delegation of nobles to the Duke to beg him to treat me well, hinting that the stability of many noble houses had depended upon my gold and my discretion. Otto pointed out that the Duke himself might need my wealth and esoteric knowledge someday. The Duke apparently made no reply, but breathed hard and walked away.

Yet while the great lords plotted and debated, other men, lesser, unnoticed men, were taking action. The Bishop had reported the ritual murder slander to the Holy See, and his dutiful secretary had made multiple copies of this detailed epistle. A poor country friar, who had always viewed the Jews with suspicion, somehow saw the report. This friar then stormed the countryside preaching that a Jew who had abandoned his people's pernicious, lying faith had attempted to expose the truth: Two innocent Christian children had been the victims of Jewish ritual murder, but the Duke and the Bishop were conspiring to conceal the crimes and to protect the murderers. The friar thundered for justice in town after town.

The peasants went wild with fury. In some towns, the Duke's men were able to protect the local Jews in His Excellency's citadels. But in others, the mob dragged Jews from their homes—men, women, small children, old people, even babies—and beat and murdered them. Jewish homes were burned all over the Duchy.

No longer would the Jews limp along in their humble but tolerable mediocrity. They screamed in anguish at their unjust deaths—and now the Messiah would have to hear these laments, now Israel's suffering would finally be great enough to force him to act.

VII. The Silence of Heaven

RABBI JUDAH STARED out the window of his room in the fortress of the wicked one, Joseph della Reina, grateful for the silence of the night.

I am alone with my soul in the darkness, the rabbi reflected. When good Jews, the righteous of their generation, lost their lives for *kiddush ha-Shem*, the sanctification of the Holy Name, because of the wicked one's calumnies, they must have experienced this calm too: the pain and the screaming and the horrible murderers' faces must have faded away, and, for a moment, the martyrs would be alone with their souls awaiting the Angel of Death. Time would have stopped for them. Of course, soon enough they would have been brought to Paradise, to be seated upon golden thrones and waited upon by hordes of adoring angels. But before that new life in the World to Come, they must have had a brief moment, just like this, where everything stopped in the quiet gloom.

Rabbi Judah well recalled those horrible days. When the two Christian boys had been found dead, the Jews were nervous. While the Duchy had always been a safe place for its Jews, and the Duke was an honorable and just prince, who knew what dangerous slanders could be spurred on by a parent's grief? The Duke's summons had only heightened their fears. Rabbi Judah had been part of the small delegation dispatched to meet with the Duke and the Bishop. The other Jews fasted and prayed in their towns' synagogues, begging the Holy One, Blessed be He, to protect Israel from its enemies.

The rabbi's body tensed as he thought back to that journey. There had been three of them, all mighty scholars, in the carriage. No one had spoken. His two colleagues furiously swayed and chanted over the holy books they had brought along on the journey. But he had been unable to concentrate on matters of Torah. Instead, his restless eyes were lured to the window of the carriage, where the sun shone gloriously upon the golden fields. A bare-chested man and his sons were working in one of these rich fields, smiling and laughing under a puffy cloud floating in a sky endlessly wide and joyously blue.

Then came the most shameful moment of Rabbi Judah's life. Looking at the beauty bursting forth in the world around him, so indifferent to the perils facing the holy community of Israel, he had seethed with rage. How could the Holy One, Blessed be He, be silent at this terrible hour? How could He let His world parade its loveliness when Jewish lives hung so dangerously in the balance? Where was the furious thunder and raging storm of divine vengeance?

When they arrived at the castle the three rabbis were ushered into the Duke's great hall, a cavernous room with a high stone ceiling. There were no candles lit, and the sunlight peered in weakly through the narrow window slits. The Duke sat enthroned on his high perch. The only other person in the room with the three Torah scholars was Bishop Conrad, who stood next to them.

The Duke explained that an evil apostate in his court, a wealthy merchant of some sort, had claimed the Jews had murdered two Christian children to drain their blood for making matzo, identifying such-and-such telltale markings on the corpses. The Bishop had come to the defense of the Jews and denounced the accusation as a horrible lie. But the Duke, to put his mind at ease, wanted to hear directly from the learned scholars of the Jews about the relevant Jewish practices and beliefs.

Rabbi Judah stood silently as the leader of the delegation, an old man with sunken eyes and a neatly brushed white beard, praised the Duke for his wise and just rule and gently explained Jewish condemnation of murder, abhorrence of blood, and the regulations for making matzo.

The Duke listened intently. He said he found the Jews' arguments to be finely stated and well-reasoned but he did not understand why the apostate would spread such a terrible lie. And would not the apostate have known the practices of the Jews from having grown up amongst them?

The old scholar replied that, while some apostates had become genuinely convinced of the truth of the Christian faith, others were foul men whose depraved conduct had made them outcasts in their own community. Such men often exploited the goodwill of pious Christians by converting and then trying to manipulate the sympathies of their new coreligionists to avenge past insults to their honor. How well, he asked the Duke, do you truly know this apostate? We have heard that this apostate is from Spain and met Your Lordship in Italy. Can you truly know how he conducted himself before his baptism?

The Duke nodded and promised to protect his Jewish subjects from these vicious slanders. The rabbis pressed for the apostate's banishment, but the Duke hesitated and could not bring himself to speak ill of the gentleman.

On their journey back, Rabbi Judah had cried in shame at his doubts of the Holy One's love and protection for His people Israel and begged Him for forgiveness for his earlier sinful ruminations. When violence erupted against the Duchy's Jews a few weeks later, Rabbi Judah was certain his lapse of faith had been the cause and nearly starved himself to death in penitential fasting and prayer.

The rabbi's town had been under the direct control of the Bishop, whose armed guards safeguarded the Jews from the mobs of would-be murderers. Yet, he spoke to many refugees who had fled from elsewhere in the Duchy. One man told Rabbi Judah how he had hidden in an attic from which, out of a small window, he watched as his wife was dragged to the middle of the town square, shorn of her clothes and tied to a pole. Their children—three little girls, the oldest only seven years old—were murdered in front of her, their blood smeared on her naked body. Use your own children's blood, not ours, you filthy, murdering Jew, they yelled at her, you will not oppress and terrorize good Christians any longer.

And now, sleepless in that same wicked apostate's villa, the rabbi remembered those terrible days as he stared out upon the peaceful black night. Perhaps, he wondered, the wicked one is right, and Israel's suffering had been ordained by the Holy One, Blessed be He, in order to bring about the great miracle

of the coming of the Messiah. But what sins had been committed to merit such a dreadful punishment? Rabbi Judah
sighed, impatient for the day when his turn would come to be
lifted from the still night into Paradise, where all these matters
would be made clear to him at last, and the martyrs would bask
in their glory on golden thrones.

VIII. Decrees from the Upper Realms

STANDING ONCE MORE by the bedside of the wicked one, Joseph della Reina, Rabbi Judah could readily discern that the dying man's sickness had continued to worsen. One of his eyes was so covered in twitching boils leaking yellow pus that the lid was effectively sealed shut. His words were now barely audible; the rabbi's ear was forced to lean down closely towards the wicked one's mouth. But this brought the rabbi's nose close to that mouth, which emitted a hideous rotting odor from inside the wasting body.

Yet the wicked one was determined to continue his tale:

Now, Rabbi Judah, my quest could move forward in mighty leaps and bounds. Various forged versions of Bishop Conrad's letter circulated far and wide, spreading my calumnies against the holy community of Israel. My words set fire to Jewish homes across Christendom. At last, Israel's enemies had what they yearned for—proof, from the mouth of one born a Jew, that the Jews engaged in monstrous, criminal rites and preyed upon their innocent neighbors. Soon these enemies of

Israel flocked to me, here in this fortress and in this tower where we are now, to hear the libels from my own lips. And I did not disappoint them: not only tales of ritual murder, but also stealing and desecrating the holy Christian communion host, robbing and cheating through usury and bribing great lords and churchmen to look the other way. I swore the Talmud expressly sanctioned, indeed encouraged, these very crimes against good Christians and taught hatred of their Savior and his doctrine of love.

My vicious words swam into eager ears. My visitors—usually poor friars with grinding teeth and burning eyes—longed to hear more and more. Their insatiable appetite for tales of how Jews exploited and injured the Christian populace tired out even me, and, unable to conjure even more slanders, I finally sent them away. But they too spread my words far and wide, and these words lit more fires of persecution and destruction across so many holy Jewish communities.

I know it upsets you to hear these things, but you must always bear in mind that I have acted out of necessity. So long as the righteous Christians—like the Duke, like the Bishop—believed that their Jewish neighbors were humble and pious, Israel's suffering could never reach the deafening howl needed to summon the Messiah into action. And without the Messiah, every human being's life is a march toward tragedy: hunger, disease, suffering, death, all eventually devour every one of us. If only the pious Jews were slaughtered in great enough numbers, so many Isaacs under the knife on Mount Moriah, that sacrifice would melt His hardened heart and He would send his Messiah to redeem mankind.

Despite all the mad chaos I wreaked, though, the Messiah still would not reveal himself. I had dived deep into the abyss of sin—I had committed, I knew, terrible crimes—all because these were the conditions that the Messiah, in his arrogant disdain for the suffering in the world, had set for the redemption of humanity. And even so, he stayed aloof. Why? I screamed in fury. How much worse can Israel's persecution become? I knew every synagogue was filled with fasting and prayer, begging, beseeching redemption from Israel's exile and suffering.

I placed my mask upon my face and summoned her again, to this very room where you stand now. She stood by this bed, and asked me what assistance was needed.

I thundered at her: I have pursued my quest valiantly, I have raised Israel's suffering to a horrible pitch. So, where is the Messiah? Why has he not come? Answer me.

The masked lady said, with perfect calm: The time has not yet come.

I could not bear these smug, distant words—how could my efforts have not yet made the time come? Was that not the point of everything I had done? In despair, I renounced my quest. I swore to expose my own lies, and to use my wealth to rebuild the communities of Israel's remnant in exile.

She did not respond to my threat.

What are you? I demanded to know. Are you an angel or a demon?

She replied: I am the one who saved you and who lifted you up. I am the one in whom you chose to have faith.

I reached for an object—whatever my hand could find—and threw it at her. But the object vanished into the air as it approached her body.

Demon! I shouted. You are a vile deceiver, you have tricked me.

She then approached me with measured steps, and placed her finger on my lips. It was so soft and fragrant, and the rage in my heart faded away. She stroked my hair and my cheek with her other hand. It is all too much for you now, she said. You should rest. The strength in my limbs gently ebbed away, and soon I was in a deep sleep.

When I woke the next morning, my mask had disappeared, along with the Purse of Fortunatus. It was not long afterwards that the boils sprouted on my skin, and phlegm flooded my chest. My temples pounded, my forehead burned and I could not walk without being propped up. I prayed for her to return to me or for another sign from the higher realms, but there was only silence.

This was my punishment. I had been entrusted by the Holy One, Blessed be He, through His mysterious angel, with the awful task of destroying the world with a new Flood so that it could be reborn in the Messianic Age as perfect, as free from sin and death as the Garden of Eden had been before Adam and Eve's terrible sin. I had been saved from death because He had hoped that I, alone among all the men of Israel, would have the courage to immerse myself deeply enough in wickedness to force the redemption and thereby end all suffering. But my courage and faith had failed me, so I was now to forfeit the gifts of life and wealth that had been bestowed upon me. I lacked the strength and patience to pursue my crimes to the necessary conclusion. So I have failed, and thus death and suffering must continue.

My flesh will not hold out much longer. Please, Rabbi, I beg you, tell my family of my righteous mission and say *Kaddish* for my blackened soul, which I have willingly sacrificed for the sake of Israel's ultimate salvation.

The wicked one strained to remain awake to hear an answer from the rabbi, but soon collapsed into sleep again. Rabbi Judah looked at his withered, pockmarked body and shed quiet tears.

That evening, the wicked one's armed men rustled Rabbi Judah back into the black carriage and drove him home. Outside the carriage windows the moonlight illuminated silhouettes of trees and houses and fields, all serene and lovely to gaze upon. The exhausted rabbi raised prayers of thanksgiving to the Holy One, Blessed be He, for his deliverance from the mad, evil persecutor of Israel.

IX. The Last Persecution

RABBI JUDAH LEARNED of the wicked one's death while sitting quietly in the *bet midrash*, staring at a page of a holy book, but unable to muster the strength to understand what the faded Hebrew letters were trying to tell him. Shrieks of joy roused him from his stupor, although the smiling, dancing Jews around the rabbi felt far away from his sad, dreamy soul.

A distinguished householder placed a silver cup filled with wine into the rabbi's hands. Rejoice, Judah! Your tormenter has died. First, the Holy One, Blessed be He, delivered you from that wicked Haman's clutches and now the murderer has been dispatched to his just reward in the World to Come! Maybe these are signs that the pains of our long exile will be eased at last. May the Messiah come, speedily and in our days, amen, *selah*.

Yet, Rabbi Judah did not drink from the cup, but pushed it away. Keeping his silence, he stood, sighed and walked off to be alone with his thoughts. The revelers paid him no mind.

Away the rabbi strolled until he reached the town's outskirts, then a forest, and finally an abandoned ruin of an ancient

Roman fort. This spot had been a comfort since his return from the wicked one's custody. A broken wall served as a makeshift bench. Facing the rabbi from inside the ruin was an idol, a statue of some goddess from pre-Christian times, worshipped perhaps by the evil Romans who had once ruled in these German lands as they had ruled in holy Jerusalem, where they had destroyed the Temple and driven the Jews into this endless exile.

Rabbi Judah had felt uneasy since his return to the town. There had been outbursts of joy and bountiful celebratory dinners upon his sudden arrival home, and many prayers of thanksgiving soared from the town's synagogue to the Throne of Glory. All these good Jews, who looked to him for guidance, felt they knew what had been asked of them: to obey the laws of the Torah with love in their hearts, and to keep faith that the Holy One, Blessed be He, would eventually take pity upon His people Israel and bring the Messiah to redeem them. While Rabbi Judah's faith had not wavered, he felt a strange hesitancy now to act and to teach, as if the air had suddenly turned pitch black—like the plague of darkness the Holy One had brought upon the wicked Egyptians—and he had to grope forward, like a blind man, terrified of tripping over.

The celebrations faded away soon enough into the humdrum busyness of everyday life—things to buy, things to sell, foods to eat, questions about whether this or that animal was kosher, legal disputes between merchants to mediate. But it all seemed so futile now. The wicked one's words had struck him harshly: Every human life is a tragedy, a longer or shorter yet always inevitable tumble to decay, sickness, and death. Each day's petty worries were simply distractions from the unavoidable suffering that was to come. Could all this misery be averted? The Holy One had created this world with its suffering and pain, and He could change it at His will anytime. But His ways were inscrutable, and beyond Rabbi Judah's too limited human understanding. That wicked one, Joseph della Reina, had shown what horror comes from trying to hasten the end.

Many people had asked Rabbi Judah to tell of his ordeal. Had the wicked one tortured him? Threatened him? Tried to baptize him?

No, the rabbi replied, he was a weak, ill man. He only wanted my ears to attend to his last memories and wishes.

Then what did you discuss? they asked. Was he trying to repent?

He never repented. His thoughts were confused, and he raved about phantoms from his distant past that haunted his dreams. Please, I am tired, no more questions.

Rabbi Judah had mulled whether to reach out to the wicked one's family in Toledo. If they were still alive, the wicked one's parents would be bent with age, and perhaps his brothers too. Must they be burdened with the knowledge that their beloved son and brother had abandoned the faith of his forefathers and gleefully spread murderous lies about his fellow Jews?

If this even was his family. The whole tale had been suffused with madness. Maybe this family was merely another of the sick man's fevered dreams.

So, in the end, the rabbi sent no letters or inquiries to the holy community of Israel in Toledo, Spain.

Sitting again now in the ruins of the ancient Roman fort in the forest, his eyes fell upon the thick old trees that, he reflected, probably were in the exact same spot when the building held soldiers homesick for the Italian countryside. Rabbi Judah wondered whether the world would have less pain and rage if everyone could humbly submit to His inscrutable decree that every human physical life would eventually be snuffed out in an undeserved agony of sickness and death. The Messianic Age would no doubt be glorious, but who could imagine what that world would be like? It is beyond us and our limited minds. We should be thankful to have been blessed with the holy Torah to guide us through this world, which He chose to create.

The sky darkened and the wind gathered up pellets of rain and whipped them into Rabbi Judah's face and hands. To shield himself from the storm, he crouched underneath the broken stone wall and looked up at the old idol. He marveled how, unlike the rest of the weed-infested, crumbling fort, the statue of the goddess had managed to remain intact with its luster undiminished.

The storm grew worse, and the wind howled about the ruin. The rabbi grew apprehensive. The idol's eyes, barely visible with the dark clouds blocking the sun, seemed to bore intensely into his own, which he reflexively closed to protect himself.

After a few moments he could tell, despite his shut eyes, that some new light had entered the remains of the fort. Perhaps the storm is easing, he thought, so the rabbi opened his eyes and sat up. The light, he now saw, came from within the statue. Quick prayers flew across his lips begging for the protection of the Holy One, Blessed be He, from whatever demon was haunting this cursed place.

The statue acquired the color of a human woman, and began to move. To his horror, the rabbi beheld a beautiful, tall

woman in a clinging silk dress with long, loose black hair and
an expressionless, pale carnival mask about her face. She
walked over until she stood towering above his shivering,
soaked body.

She sighed gently and addressed him in a sweet, soothing
voice:

Dear Rabbi Judah ben Gershom: That is no way to greet
someone who has come to help you. And not from this
storm—the storm will soon pass, but then your real troubles
shall arrive. You have met my dear friend, Joseph della Reina,
who has so recently passed into the next world. He was once
shivering in a terrible storm, too, until I saved him.

Your life is in grave danger. A rumor has spread that,
during your private discussions with the late Joseph, you poi-
soned him. This is not true—I had withdrawn my protection
from him and the death that had been foreordained for him
long ago was then able to creep back again into his flesh. Yet,
unfortunately, Joseph had taught so many of them that there is
no calamity without a wicked, dirty Jew at its root.

They are arming now, these enemies of yours, and mean
to sever your head from your neck. Who knows what else they
may do? Burn your synagogue and its holy texts? Butcher your
grandchildren? Maybe even travel up and down the Rhine kill-
ing Jews wherever they happen to find them?

You can stop them. I have a magical purse, which brings
forth a limitless abundance of gold coins. Use it to bribe Count
Otto and his retainers to protect you. Since I withdrew my favor from Joseph, Otto has been unable to fund his gambling
debts and mistresses. You can be the new banker paying for
the sins of the great nobles of the Duchy of W., and they in

turn will protect you. Reach out your hand now. Let me give the Purse of Fortunatus to you.

The rabbi curled into a tight ball, shut his eyes and moaned heartfelt prayers to the higher realms.

I see you need time to consider the situation. Very well, tonight, under your pillow, you will find your carnival mask. Place it upon your face to summon me to return.

The rabbi sat with his eyes shut for several more minutes. When he opened them again, the masked lady was gone, and before him was again only the white marble statue of the ancient fort's goddess.

That evening ill tidings reached the town's Jewish quarter. A friendly monk, who did business with local Jewish merchants, relayed that Rabbi Judah had been accused of poisoning the wicked one, and that the dead man's friends and retainers were arming for revenge.

Rabbi Judah did not know what to do. In the twilight, he walked anxiously through the Jewish quarter, and there they all were: cranky children grousing after a long day of *cheder,* squat women sighing after a day of washing, cooking, and mending, merchants with a nervous edge, eager for the next opportunity, and melancholy artisans, who dreamed of the days when Israel's exile would end and the Messiah would gift each Jew with his own orange grove in the Holy Land.

Now they were all to be snuffed out, like so many useless candles that had poured too much light into a room. So what to do? They could seek safety with the Bishop's garrison in the citadel and chance that the local detachment would be strong and brave enough to resist the invaders. But if the Bishop was not on their side, they would be rushing into the arms of death.

They could flee, but their pursuers would overtake them, especially the very old and the very young.

Rabbi Judah entered his house, and walked through the narrow hallway to his bed chamber in the rear. No one else was present. With trembling hands, he reached underneath his pillow and felt something hard, but softer than stone or metal. He pulled it out.

In his hands was an Italian carnival mask, stark white except for the eyes, which were painted blue and the exaggerated, hooked nose, which was red. Feeling chilled and light-headed, the rabbi placed the strange object into his satchel and went outside again.

The night was warm but not humid, with a wide dark blue sky lit by a half moon. Birds sang and insects hummed, and alone in the forest the rabbi found it hard to believe that the world could be so cruel and dangerous. The broken wall of the ruined fort rose before him again, and he sat down facing the marble idol of the wicked Romans' goddess.

Rabbi Judah took the mask out of his satchel and looked at it closely. Feeling a surge of anger, in his heart he bitterly accused the Holy One, Blessed be He, of horrible injustice for letting the wicked idolaters murder innocent Jews again and again throughout so many centuries of miserable exile.

These bitter thoughts were an echo, he realized, of something he had read before, of different yet similar words uttered in outrage in the distant past: They were the accusations of the righteous Job, denouncing the Holy One for unjustly afflicting him with suffering and murdering his family.

But then the rabbi recalled the words of the Holy One, Blessed be He, addressed to Job from the awesome whirlwind, holding in contempt the notion that a puny thing like a mortal man could judge what is so beyond his limited faculties.

And without realizing it, Rabbi Judah began to utter aloud words so similar to Job's reply to the Holy One's admonishment: I am small, I am worthless, I am dust and ashes, I have only heard rumor of You, but I have never beheld You in Your true infinite splendor, I retract and I recant.

Rabbi Judah walked to the statue and roared three Hebrew words into her masked eyes: *Baruch dayan emet*—blessed is the Righteous Judge. He threw the mask upon the ground and stomped upon it with his foot. The rabbi felt tears of joy engulf his face as he walked slowly home in the tranquil night.

Other Books by Barak Bassman

Elegy of the Minotaur

Repentance: A Tale of Demons in Old Jewish Poland

King Solomon and Ashmedai: A Wisdom Tale

The Twilight of the Magical Siren: A Tale of Late Antiquity

The Leper Princess and The Court Jew

www.ingramcontent.com/pod-product-compliance
Lightning Source LLC
Chambersburg PA
CBHW032022180726
48283CB00008B/2791